AT THE EDGE
OF THE WORLD
Stewart Ross

CONTENTS

TO THE READER

At the edge of the world takes place in Greenland and North America over 1,000 years go. Leif, his father Erik the Red, and most of the other characters are real; a few, like Nansun the Navigator, are made up. The setting is also real and the voyages across the North Atlantic actually happened. By telling them as a story, I have tried to bring to life one of the most exciting adventures of all time.

Stewart Ross

THE STORY SO FAR ...

People who knew how to farm came to Britain more than 6,000 years ago. They kept animals and grew crops in fields they cleared in the forests. Their tools were made of wood, stone, bone, and soft metals such as copper. We call this period of history the Neolithic Era.

These early Britons must have been well-organized because they built large monuments, such as tombs and temples. The most famous is Stonehenge, the construction of which began around 3500 BCE. The first stones were raised on the site 1,000 years later.

By this time, a very important change was taking place. Neolithic people found that by mixing copper with a little tin they produced a much harder and tougher metal called bronze. This was used to make better tools, such as axes, and stronger weapons, like swords.

Tin and copper were found in Britain, especially in the southwest, and the people of this region became expert miners. They also grew rich because traders from all over Europe travelled to Britain to exchange their fine cloth, jewellery and other goods for British metal. The journey was made in large wooden boats powered by sails or by rows of paddles.

At the time of our story, about 2100 BCE, we believe Britons lived in tribes, each under a powerful leader.

The members of a tribe worked together on building projects and almost certainly waged war on other tribes.

TIME LINE

CE (Common Era)

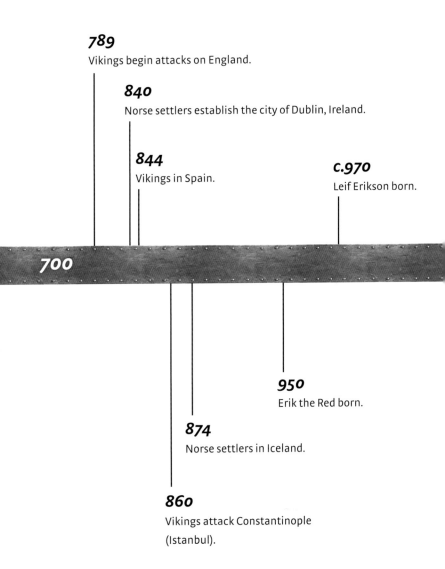

789
Vikings begin attacks on England.

840
Norse settlers establish the city of Dublin, Ireland.

844
Vikings in Spain.

c.970
Leif Erikson born.

700

950
Erik the Red born.

874
Norse settlers in Iceland.

860
Vikings attack Constantinople (Istanbul).

981
Erik the Red discovers Greenland.

C.1000
Leif Erikson travels to
Norway.

1492
Christopher Columbus 'discovers'
the New World.

C.1003
Erik the Red dies.

1016
Cnut, a Dane, becomes King of England.

1500

C. 1020
Leif Erikson dies.

1010
Viking explorers settle
in North America.

C.1002-3
Leif Erikson explores the coast of North America.

Chapter 1

THE CHALLENGE

'Old?' thundered Erik the Red, glaring round the hall. 'If anyone dares call me old, I'll slice them up and feed the bits to the seagulls! By Thor's great hammer, I will!'

He took another long swig of mead and rose to his feet. Tall, red-bearded and covered in battle scars, he was a terrifying sight. 'And if anyone thinks I'm joking,' he snorted, grasping the hilt of his huge sword, 'let them try me! Come on! I'm ready!'

For a time, the only sound was the crackling of the pine logs blazing in the hearth at the centre of hall. Eventually, a calm voice cut through the silence.

'Please sit down, father. You're making everyone nervous.' It was Leif, Erik the Red's eldest son. Only he dared challenge the wrath of his ferocious father.

As Erik turned and stared at him, the warrior's weather-beaten face glowed in the firelight. Never had the nickname 'the Red' suited him better.

'You?' growled the veteran of a dozen deadly fights. 'My own son didn't call me old, did he?'

'No, father. I simply said you had seen many years. Half a hundred I believe it is?'

'Maybe,' sniffed Erik. 'And I've done more in that time than a dozen ordinary men.'

A woman now spoke. 'There you go, husband –

boasting again!' It was Hilda, Erik's wife and mother of his four children.

'Be quiet, woman!' snapped Erik. 'This is men's business.'

A low murmur ran through the hall. Now they were Christian, the people of Greenland were trying to change the way women were treated. But Erik was a Viking of the old school. He had refused to accept Christianity and its new-fangled, kindly attitudes. Kindness, he swore, was a sign of weakness.

Hilda would not be silenced so easily. 'All right then, husband,' she said, 'let's have a competition.'

When Erik tried to interrupt her, she raised her hand. 'Listen, for once! You say you've done more than a dozen other men. Well, I say our son Leif has done more in his thirty years than you have in your fifty!'

'Never!' roared Erik, drawing his sword and brandishing it above his head. 'And I'll prove it in a fight!'

Hilda sighed and shook her head. 'Fighting will prove nothing, husband. In the end, words always beat blades. So please put your sword away and tell everyone about the wonderful things you've done.'

She pointed to an old man seated on a stool close the fire. 'Olaf the Wise, would you kindly act as our judge?'

Olaf raised his head, looked at Erik, then at Leif, and nodded. 'I will, Lady Hilda.'

'Thank you, Olaf.' Hilda turned to Erik. 'So, husband, the floor is yours. We are all ears. Let's hear of your great deeds.'

The huge Viking strode to a space beside the hearth and ran his eyes over the throng of warriors, farmers, mothers, children, and lowly thralls. 'I am surprised,' he began, 'that you need me to remind you of what I have done. But obviously you have short memories, so I'll tell you again.

'Let me begin with what I am most proud of. I have slain many men.'

At the back of the hall, a number of thralls shifted uncomfortably.

'You don't like that? Listen! We are Vikings! We live under the eyes of the great gods – they are watching to see which of us is like them. The mighty Odin, father of all the gods, is a warrior. His great son Thor, the sender of thunder, is a warrior. Even Hel, the monster ruler of the Land of the Dead, is a warrior.

'As they slay their enemies, so should we. And if we ourselves die in battle, the gods will welcome us to their home, Valhalla.

Erik's voice rose to tremendous roar. 'You hear me? Of all of you, listen to what I'm saying: I – am – like – a – god!'

Chapter 2

ERIKLAND!

The phrase 'like a god' brought gasps of surprise and dismay from the audience. Some of the older men, warriors who had sailed the seas with Erik and fought beside him in battle, nodded in agreement. But most of the others frowned in disapproval.

Though Greenland had been a Christian community for only a couple of years, the majority of its inhabitants now accepted that there was just one God. No human being – not even Erik the Red – could be like Him.

'So you don't like what I say?' Erik continued, taking another gulp of mead. 'Well, bad luck! There's more to come.'

He pointed a craggy finger at a young man sitting opposite him. 'You, Arvid Gunterson, what land do you live in?'

Arvid looked around nervously. 'Er, this one, Lord Erik.'

'I know that, you tadpole! What's it called?'

'Greenland.'

'Well done! And who gave it that name?'

Arvid smiled weakly. 'You did, Lord Erik.'

'Exactly! I found this land. I named this land. I settled this land with boatloads of people from Iceland and Norway. You know how many families live here now? About a thousand!

'Think about it... I made this place. It shouldn't be called Greenland, should it? It ought to be Erikland!'

A ripple of laughter swept the hall.

'There you have it, fellow Vikings! Are you going to tell me that my son Leif – noble though he is – has done half as much as me, Erik the Red?'

With that, the famous old Viking sat down and drained his pot of mead.

'And now,' said Olaf the Wise, 'we shall hear from Leif Erikson. Tell us, Leif, what have you achieved in your thirty years?'

Leif shared many of his father's looks. The same square shoulders, strong arms and clear blue eyes. But there were striking differences. The father's voice was as rough as the Atlantic waves; the son's softer, more musical. Erik's hair was the colour of the sunset, Leif's resembled summer corn. Where Erik's lips twisted into a snarl, his son's played closer to a smile.

All his life Erik had made enemies and enjoyed taking them on; Leif preferred friendships. While nearly everybody crammed into the wooden hall on that cold winter's night was afraid of Erik the Red, they all had a place in their hearts for his son.

How had father and son turned out so different? Surely Erik had raised his son in his own image, teaching him the ways of war, bloodshed and revenge? No. Erik the Red had shown no interest in his children. He was too busy on his adventures to spend time on what he called 'women's work' at home.

The biggest influences on the young Leif were not his father but his mother, Hilda, and Tyrker the Thrall. Little more than a household slave, Tyrker had been a sort of foster father to Leif. He accompanied the lad wherever he went, and taught him to how to snare rabbits and how to catch rich salmon in the fast-flowing rivers.

Above all, Tyrker the Thrall taught Leif that the only important thing in life was not *who* a person was but *what* they were.

'I am proud of my father,' Leif began when he got up to speak. 'Very proud. I cannot compete with him in many things. I have not quarrelled like him, I have not fought like him, and I have not killed like him.'

At this, Erik gave a loud snort and called for more drink.

Leif ignored him and went on, 'But I have done other things. I have travelled to Norway and sat in the court of the mighty King Olaf. There I met with merchants from lands I had never before heard of, lands where kings live in palaces with roofs of beaten gold, and the ladies wear diamonds and rubies as large as hailstones.'

On every side, Leif's audience sat in open-mouthed wonder.

'And there, amid all the splendour and glory of the Norwegian court, I heard news that changed my life – and yours – for ever.'

Chapter 3

OCEAN AND MORE OCEAN

'You know what my news was,' Leif continued, speaking slowly and quietly. 'It was the good news. The news about the One God and his Son, Jesus Christ.'

'There you go again!' scoffed Erik. 'Really, Leif, we've had enough of all this Jesus nonsense. Love your neighbour? Ha! You won't catch me loving my neighbour if he nicks my cows. I'll chop his head off!'

Olaf the Wise raised a hand. 'Lord Erik, your son didn't interrupt when you were speaking, so please don't interrupt him.'

'Alright, Olaf. I'll let him have his say.'

Leif thanked his father and explained how he had brought the Christian message from Norway to Greenland. The people had listened to him and nearly all agreed to become Christian. As he was saying this, Leif looked at his father and shook his head. Erik grinned, and sipped his mead.

'So I have brought a better, truer way of life to Greenland,' Leif went on. 'A way of life that will, I hope, save your souls.'

When one or two people cried, 'hear-hear!' Leif held up his hand for silence. 'Thank you, but I have something else to say. Instead of killing people, with God's help I have rescued them.

'As you know, during my voyage back here from Norway, we were blown off course. Far off course. Great green waves tossed our ship about like a leaf; gales bent the mast like a bow; and for days on end we drifted in icy fog so thick we couldn't see from one end of the boat to the other.

'Thankfully, God was with us, and we survived. But when we came within sight of the coast, it was not a land we recognised. It was a strange place, thick with forests. A land at the edge of the world. And on the shore in that lonely place we found two of our men, Greenlanders.

'Yes, you know who they were. Gunnar Sigurdson and Uffe Adesson. They had been sailing with Bjarni Herjolfson when they were shipwrecked on that empty coast.'

Leif turned and pointed to two men sitting on the floor behind him. 'We rescued them, brought them safe back home – and here they are, fit and well!'

Erik scowled as the audience murmured 'yes!' and 'well done!'

'So that is what I have to say,' Leif concluded. 'I have saved where my father killed. And I have done my best to save bodies as well as souls.'

'Hold on!' cried Erik, jumping to his feet. 'Before we go any further, there's something I'd like to add. That alright, Olaf?'

The old man frowned and looked at Leif. 'Do you mind?'

Leif shrugged. 'No, of course not.'

'Good,' said Erik. 'What I want to know is this: how do we know any of this is true, eh?'

Leif looked puzzled. 'Know what is true, father?'

'All this talk of a land at the edge of the world. Everyone knows that beyond Greenland it's just ocean and more ocean. There's no land out there. If you ask me, you picked up Gunnar and Uffe from Iceland and made up the shipwreck story.'

'Why would I do that?'

'Because you wanted to show that this god of yours is more powerful than Odin, that's why. It's nonsense!'

'No it's not, Lord Erik! I swear that we did indeed see a new world.' All heads turned towards an elderly man standing in the corner of the hall beside his wife. It was Bjarni Herjolfson.

'So you're in on this plot, Bjarni?' growled Erik the Red. 'Don't tell me... you've fallen for this Christian rubbish, eh?'

'Jesus Christ came to save us,' said Bjarni.

'Great Odin's bloody beard!' thundered Erik. 'What's got into you lot? Where's the Viking in you?'

When no one answered, Hilda said, 'Husband, all this shouting is getting you nowhere. Olaf the Wise can't decide between you and Leif until you've seen for yourself the place where Gunnar and Uffe were shipwrecked. Then you'll know for certain your son is telling the truth.'

'What do you mean, woman?'

'I mean this, husband: if this land at the edge of the world really does exist, then why not ask Leif to take you there?'

Chapter 4

THE REJECTION

Erik the Red accepted his wife's idea immediately.

'Now we'll see what that son of mine is made of!' he chuckled when the couple were alone. 'He's a good sailor, I'll grant him that. But sailing into emptiness... That takes guts!'

'It does,' agreed Hilda. 'But perhaps it'd be more sensible to ask one of your friends to sail with Leif rather than go yourself? After all, at your age –'

'My age!? Don't you start, woman. I'm as strong as any of them. No, stronger. Besides, if I don't go myself, they'll only invent some Christian lie about their goddle mighty guiding them?'

And that was the end of the conversation.

Not far away, in another corner of the Brattalid settlement, Leif was holding a conversation of his own. He lived in a large hall-house with stone walls and a timber roof covered with thatch, turf and slabs of flat stone. The few farm animals kept over the winter lived at one end, and Leif, his brothers and their families lived together at the other.

During the long, dark winter, when snow often lay thick on the ground, a fire burned day and night in a stone hearth at the centre of the hut. This left the air thick with smoke, and Leif blinked to clear his eyes as he looked at his family gathered about him.

'Well,' said Thorvald, the elder of his two brothers, 'are you really going to do it, Leif?'

'Of course.'

'Why?'

Leif thought for a moment. 'Good question, Thorvald.'

'Yes, it is,' interrupted Thorgunna, Leif's wife. 'And I want to know why, too.'

'I think we all do,' added Leif's sister, Freydis. Her husband had recently vanished on a voyage from Greenland to Iceland, and she knew as well as anyone how perilous the ocean could be.

'We Norse people have always been sailors and explorers, and I want to continue that proud tradition,' Leif explained. 'Our ancestor was the first man to build a base in Iceland; my father was the first to build one here, in Greenland; and I want to be first to set up a Norse base in the land at the edge of the world.'

'For fame and glory then?' asked Thorgunna.

'Yes, partly. But I also want to show that Christians can be just as bold and brave as the old Vikings, but without the bloodshed.'

Thorvald took a deep breath. 'Sounds good, Leif. You can count me in as one of the crew.'

'And me,' said Thorstein, Leif's other brother.

'And me!' piped up Leif's eldest son, the twelve-year-old Thorgils.

Leif smiled at his wife. 'Well, Thorgunna? It's your decision. Is Thorgils old enough to come with us?'

As Thorgunna looked at her son, her eyes filled with tears.

'Please, mother!'

'Very well, you may go, Thorgils. But on one condition. Promise?'

'What is it?'

'That you come back safe and sound!'

Leif put a hand on his wife's arm. 'He will, Thorgunna. God willing.'

* * *

They spent the next few weeks planning the expedition. They had plenty of time: the winter days were still short and the waves rolling by the coast were rarely without stormy white crests.

A successful voyage required two things, a seaworthy vessel and a first-class navigator. The boat was no problem. After a bit of haggling, Bjarni sold his knarr to Leif. It had proved it's worth the previous year when it had survived the storm that had shipwrecked Gunnar and Uffe. As soon as a price was agreed, Leif and his brothers began carrying out the necessary repairs and maintenance.

Obtaining the services of an expert navigator was not so easy. Nansun, the best sailor Leif had ever known, refused point blank to join his crew.

'Nope,' he said, shaking his head. 'Sorry Leif, but my wife and I were married only a couple of weeks ago, and the last thing she wants is for me to go risking my life again on some madcap trip to the edge of the world.'

'But we couldn't go without you to guide us,' explained Leif.

'Then you'd better not go, Leif. Simple as that.'

Chapter 5

AMBER AND GOLD

Brattalid was soon buzzing with the news of Nansun's refusal.

'Not going with Leif, eh?' tutted the priest, Father Gudrun, when he was told. 'Well, I can't say I blame Nansun. He and the young Waiola were married in the sight of God. I don't suppose He'd be too pleased if Nansun sailed off into the unknown so soon.'

Father Gudrun smiled. 'And I don't suppose Waiola would be too pleased, either.'

He was right there. Nansun's wife, Waiola, might have been only sixteen, but she knew her mind alright. When she heard Leif was going to ask her husband to join the expedition, her ice-blue eyes sparkled with anger.

'Never!' she told Nansun, grasping his right hand in hers. 'If you care for me, husband, you'll not desert me like some pagan Viking of the olden days. You're a man, aren't you? Not a monster!'

Nansun was dearly fond of his wife, and could not say no to her. Three times Leif asked him to join his crew, and three times the celebrated navigator said no. When he heard what was going on, Erik the Red roared with laughter and slapped his thigh.

'I was right, woman!' he scoffed when Hilda asked what all the noise was about. 'That land Leif and

Bjarni talk about doesn't exist. They invented it so they could say they'd found somewhere new, like I found Greenland. Now Nansun's refused to help, they daren't even try to sail there!'

Thorgunna, Leif's wife, was as upset as her husband when she heard of Nansun's decision. 'Have you any idea why?' she asked.

'Yes. He doesn't want to leave Waiola so soon after their marriage,' said Leif.

Thorgunna thought for a moment. 'Is it because he doesn't want to leave her, or because she doesn't want him to go?'

'Probably a bit of both. But from what he said, it sounded as if she has ordered him not to go.'

'Let me try, husband,' smiled Thorgunna.

'You really think Nansun will listen to you?'

'Of course not. But it's not him I'm going to talk to.'

* * *

Thorgunna and Waiola met a few days later. Waiola was returning from the little wooden church Leif had built when he and Father Gudrun returned from Norway with the Christian message. Thorgunna had been watching for Waiola and trudged out into the snow pretending she needed to collect firewood.

'Hello,' she said cheerily. 'Been to the church?'

'Hello Thorgunna. Yes, I've been to thank God for giving me such a fine husband.'

The older woman smiled. 'Indeed, Nansun's a great man. "Nansun the Navigator" they call him – best there is.'

'I'm so proud of him.'

Thorgunna looked around at the snowy landscape. 'How do you think he'll take to farming?'

'What?'

'Farming. You know, ploughing, milking cows and all that sort of thing.'

'Oh, you won't catch him doing that!' laughed Waiola. 'He's a sailor.'

'Of course he is, my dear. And his skills will earn enough to buy you the finest jewellery in Greenland. The snow's beginning to melt, which means it shouldn't be long before the first merchant ship arrives from Norway.'

An odd look came over Waiola's face.

'The merchant I met last year said he'd be coming back with a necklace of amber on a gold chain. It'd look beautiful on you, Waiola. You must get Nansun to buy it for you. Probably no more than half a pound of silver.'

The young woman blushed. 'I – I don't think he could afford it,' she stammered. 'We've only got a few old coins.'

Thorgunna rested her hand on Waiola's arm. 'Don't worry, my dear. I'm sure Nansun will make a fortune selling vegetables.'

'But he won't be growing vegetables! As I told you, Thorgunna, Nansun's a sailor.'

'Of course!' Thorgunna turned to go back to the house. 'Anyway, I must go in now. Food to prepare. Lovely chatting to you. And good luck with that necklace – see if Nansun can find a way of buying it for you.'

Chapter 6

120 SILVER PENNIES

That evening, as Thorgunna and Leif were sitting beside the fire, she said, 'You know that money you brought back from Norway – the money King Olaf gave you...'

'Yes. What of it?'

'How much is left?'

'I'm not sure. I know there are three gold coins and quite a few silver ones. Perhaps a couple of pounds in weight, maybe more. Why are you asking? Do you want something from the merchant when he comes in the spring?'

'No, husband. Thank you all the same. I don't want anything, but I know someone else who does.'

'Who?'

'Wait and see, husband. Wait and see!'

* * *

Leif did not have to wait long. A week later, as he and his brothers were working on the boat, a familiar figure approached them.

'Hey, Leif, can I have a word?'

'Sure, Nansun. Have you come to lend a hand to make up for not being our navigator?'

'That's what I wanted to talk about.'

Leif was confused. 'Not being our navigator, you mean?'

Nansun took a deep breath and looked out to sea.

'Sort of. You see, I've changed my mind. I will join your expedition.'

'That's brilliant!' Leif grabbed Nansun's hand and shook it warmly.

'But I need to be paid, Leif.'

'No problem. The land we saw is covered with trees. We'll fell some and sell the wood here and in Iceland. Should fetch a good prince and –'

'I'd like to be paid now,' interrupted Nansun. 'One hundred and twenty silver pennies.'

'Hang on! Half a pound of silver? It's a small fortune.'

'The price of an amber and gold necklace.'

'What did you say?'

'Nothing. Just talking to myself. Have you got the money, Leif?'

Leif sighed. 'It's an awful lot, but I suppose so.' He put out his hand. 'Here's to the deal, Nansun.'

The two men shook hands. Smiling like a child, the Navigator went home to Waiola, and Leif returned to work beside his brothers.

'Well, what did he want?' asked Thorvald.

'I think he wants an amber and gold necklace,' grinned Leif. 'But more important than that, he's changed his mind. Nansun the Navigator is coming with us to the edge of the world.'

* * *

By the late spring, after the snow had melted, Leif's boat
was ready. They called her Fish because she slipped into
the water so easily and seemed at home there.
Leif had chosen a fine crew. He picked his family first:
Tyrker the Thrall, his brothers Thorvald and Thorsten,
his sister Freydis, and his son Thorgils, who had now
turned thirteen. The rest of the crew – four women and
nineteen men – were all experienced seafarers. But they
admitted they were novices compared with Nansun.

By just looking at the waves and sniffing the air, the
Navigator could tell the direction of the nearest land.
From the birds and the fish, he knew how far away it
was, too. He understood the currents and the winds,
the tides and the clouds. He sensed when a storm was
coming two days before it arrived.

Once Fish was in the water, the crew raised the tall
mast and fastened it in place with sealskin ropes. Then
they carried on board the huge sail, knitted over the
winter with wool sheared from Greenland sheep.

Next came the stores: wooden barrels of drinking
water, cheese and dried meat; baskets of butter, and
nets of vegetables. Finally, two sheep, a ram, a cow and
a bull were coaxed up the gangplank and tied up below
deck. If they were to stay over the winter in the strange
new land, the explorers would need farm animals.

At last, as Father Gudrun – the only literate man in
Brattalid – announced that May was about to become

June, all was ready.

All? Not quite. One crew member had not yet loaded his things on board. Erik the Red was playing it cool.

Chapter 7

DOOMED!

The night before Fish was due to sail, Leif visited his father to make sure everything was alright.

'Of course everything's alright!' cried Erik. 'An old Viking's ready at a moment's notice. All he needs is his leather coat, a bag of oats and his axe.'

Leif grinned. 'Did you say "old Viking", father?'

'Enough of your cheek, son,' Erik growled, looking redder than ever. 'I meant I was experienced, that's all. Now you get back to that ship of yours, and I'll see you at dawn – for the voyage to nowhere. Ha-ha!'

With his father's mocking laughter still in his ears, Leif said goodbye and set out for home. *I respect my father*, he thought as he crossed the meadow above his hall. *He's as brave as a bear and twice as tough. But I wish he wasn't always trying to prove himself better than everyone else.*

* * *

The following morning dawned chilly and bright. A soft breeze rippled the sea and tugged gently at Fish's sealskin rigging.

'Ideal weather,' said Leif to his brothers as they stowed away the food the crew had brought for the voyage. 'A good omen, eh?'

'God willing,' said Gunnar, one of the men Leif had rescued. Although he had been shipwrecked on the distant coast, Gunnar was keen to return. He'd seen more fine timber there, he told Leif, than in the whole of Norway. And the salmon! There were so many they practically jumped out of the rivers into your arms.

Every able-bodied person in Brattalid gathered on the shore to see the boat off. Men, women and children stood around in groups, chatting quietly. Bidding farewell to a crew embarking on a long voyage was never joyful. Expert sailors though the Vikings were, each year the angry Atlantic claimed dozens of brave lives.

Leif stood on the plank that ran from the rocky shore to his boat. Where was his father? He was starting to wonder what to do if Erik failed to turn up, when he heard horse's hooves clopping along the rocky path that led down to the shore.
There he was! Trust Erik the Red to make a spectacular last-minute arrival!

Leif watched as the horse picked its way over the rocks still slippery with dew. Erik stood up in the saddle and waved. 'Hey!' he shouted. 'Don't go without your most important passenger!'

What happened next, no one was quite sure. Maybe it was the sudden movement of the rider, or his raucous cries? For whatever reason, the horse stumbled and fell forward.

Erik had let go the reigns to wave. As he was standing up, he had no grip with his knees, either. Like a seal slipping off a rock into the sea, the old Viking slid gracefully over the horse's neck and landed with a crack on the rocky ground.

For a moment, he lay there unmoving. He then slowly clambered to his feet, grabbed the horse's reigns and stared at his son.

'You alright, father?'

'Of course I'm alright. But you aren't.'

Erik left his horse with a bystander and strode towards the shore. Leif watched him carefully. 'What do you mean by "you aren't"?' he demanded when his father was a couple of paces away.

Erik shook his head. 'You saw what happened, didn't you?'

'Of course. You fell off your horse.'

'Fell off my horse? Don't be stupid, son. I didn't fall off. I was thrown – and you know by whom, don't you?'

'No.'

'By Odin! It was a warning from the greatest of all the gods. Odin the Mighty was telling one of his heroes not to join your voyage, Leif.'

Erik stood, legs apart, and raised his right hand until it was pointing straight at the Fish.

'Hear me, sailors!' he cried in a hideous voice. 'Sail not in that vessel. She is doomed, do you hear? Doomed!'

Chapter 8

AT THE EDGE OF THE WORLD

Leif knew that if he did not act swiftly, the voyage to the land at the edge of the world really would be doomed. He also realised that he risked falling out with his father for ever.

But it had to be done.

'Friends!' he cried, looking round at the crew and the people on the shore. 'Listen to me! You have just heard the voice of the old world, the world of bloodthirsty gods and cruel superstitions.

'An elderly man fell from his horse, and to hide his embarrassment he said a god had pushed him. What nonsense!

'The One God, our God, does not push people off horses or sink boats. He loves us – that's why he sent his Son to guide us.

'I tell you, this voyage is not doomed. It is blessed!'

Leif looked straight at the priest. 'Tell me, Father Gudrun – am I right?'

For a brief moment, the priest looked anxious. Then he spread out his hands towards the Fish. 'You are indeed right, Leif. God bless this vessel and all who sail in her!' he chanted.

A wave of relief ran through Leif as the crowd clapped their hands in approval. *I've done it*, he thought as he watched his father stumble angrily away. *I have finally broken free from the control of a cruel man.*

Beside him, Nansun the Navigator sniffed the air. 'Wind's right, sea's right – all set fair for a calm voyage, Leif. Let's get going!'

* * *

And calm the voyage was. Fish sailed up the coast of Greenland before turning west towards the setting sun. Barely ten days later, they sighted land.

'There it is! On the starboard bow!' cried Nansun, peering through the morning mist at the dark shape ahead.

His shipmates stared in the direction he was pointing. 'Yes!' yelled Thorgils, glancing up at his father, his face glowing with pride. 'We've done it!'

'Not yet, son,' replied Leif. 'Not yet.'

He was right. They had certainly found land, but it didn't look like the place they remembered. The shore was flat and covered with stone slabs.

'Nothing like where I was,' muttered Gunnar. 'No trees, for a start.'

Leif turned to Nansun. 'So what happens now, Navigator?'

'Patience, Leif. You'll get your money's worth, don't worry.' He looked about him and pushed the steering oar to the right. 'Easy. We just turn south and follow the coast towards the trees and sunshine.'

Leif frowned. 'Trees and sunshine? How do you know?'

'Don't ask, Leif,' grinned Nansun. 'Just trust me.'

Down the coast they went. And, as Nansun had predicted, the weather grew warmer and the land greener. First there were great forests, then more open countryside with flowers and meadows.

Here they went ashore and pulled Fish high up on to the beach to protect her from the waves. While half the crew set about making shelters, the others went exploring. They returned with handfuls of a strange berry that no one had seen before.

'They look good,' said Freydis, Leif's sister. She put one in her mouth. 'Mmm! They taste good, too. You know what, I reckon they're grapes, the fruit that grows on vines.'

'In which case,' said Leif, tasting one of the berries himself, 'we'll call this place Vine-land.'

* * *

Five days later, when their base was well established, Leif and Tyrker the Thrall left to climb the tall hill overlooking the camp. Leif wanted to see what lay on the other side and whether there was any sign of human life.

The climb took them four hours, but it was worth it. Standing on a rocky peak, they looked around in amazement. The scene seemed to go on for ever –

woods, lakes, rivers, meadows stretching as far as the eye could see.

'Wow!' gasped Tyrker. 'It doesn't look like the land at the edge of the world does it?'

'No,' said Leif, his eyes wide with wonder. 'I don't reckon we're at the edge of our world at all. It's much more than that. I think we've discovered a whole New World.'

THE HISTORY FILE

WHAT HAPPENED NEXT?

Leif and his crew spent the winter in Vinland. In the spring they returned to Greenland with a cargo of grapes and timber. After this, Leif gave up exploring and settled down on his farm. He spent a lot of his time telling the Greenlanders about the Christian faith.

We can't be sure, but it is possible that Erik the Red died when his son was in North America. Perhaps that fall from his horse was more serious than he had admitted?

Leif's brother Thorvald led a second expedition to Vinland. His men were the first Vikings to meet with Native Americans, and there was bloody fighting between the two peoples. The Vikings never settled permanently in North America, perhaps because of hostility from those already living there. However, occasional knarrs sailed over to collect timber from the forests.

Although by 1400 contact with North America had been lost, stories about Erik the Red, Leif and his family lived on, especially in Iceland. The Italian explorer Christopher Columbus said he visited Iceland in 1477. If he did, is it possible that he heard tales of a mysterious new land in the west?

We will probably never know the answer. But we do

know that in 1492 Columbus left Spain saying he was going to Japan. He never got there, of course, because the world was much larger than he realised. And between Europe and Asia lay a whole new continent – America.

For years, people believed Columbus was the European who 'discovered' America. We now know that's not true. Brave Viking explorers had been there 400 years before.

HOW DO WE KNOW?

Historians learn about the life and times of Erik the Red and Leif Erikson in two ways. One is by reading the famous Vikings sagas; the other is by studying objects remaining from that period of history.

The Viking sagas are long stories about heroes, adventures and battles. Although exciting, the sagas are not very reliable. First, they are full of exaggeration. Second, they were learned by heart and passed down by word of mouth from generation to generation. As a result, mistakes were made, and a saga changed a little every time it was retold.

The *Greenland Saga*, which talks of journeying to the New World, was not written down until at least 200 years after Leif's death. The *Saga of Erik the Red*, first written about the same time, also talks of Leif's visit to North America. However, there are two different versions of the *Saga of Erik the Red*, each slightly different. You can see why it's almost impossible to know exactly what happened on those extraordinary voyages over 1,000 years ago.

Indeed, for a long time historians did not believe the stories of trips to Vinland. Then, in the 1960s, archaeologists discovered the remains of a Viking camp at L'Anse aux Meadows in Newfoundland, Canada. Here, at last, was scientific evidence that backed the tales told in the sagas.

Archaeology provides other evidence of the Viking

way of life. No buildings are still standing. Nevertheless, by digging in the ground archaeologists have uncovered all kinds of interesting artefacts – objects that have not rotted away, such as wooden stumps, bricks, stones, bones, coins, jewellery, and weapons. We use these to help us paint a more accurate picture of those distant but fascinating times.

NEW WORDS

Archaeology
Finding out about the past by examining ancient buildings and artefacts.

Artefact
Anything made by a human being.

Chronicle
Historical record.

Convert
Change religion.

Loot
Stolen valuables.

Manuscript
Handwritten document.

Mead
A strong, honey-flavoured drink.

Monastery
Buildings, including a church or chapel, where monks live.

Navigator
Sailor skilled at working out a ship's course across open sea.

Norseman
Man from Scandinavia.

Pagan
Believing in many gods rather than one.

Rafters
Open wooden beams holding up a roof.

Saga
A long, epic story, sometimes with bits of poetry in it.

Scandinavia
Denmark, Norway and Sweden.

Slay
Kill.

Thrall
A slave.

Thor
The Viking God of Thunder.

Throng
A crowd.

Timber
Wood.

Turf
Grass and the soil on which it grows.

Valhalla
The giant hall where the Viking gods were said to live.

Vikings
The warlike people of Scandinavia who attacked Western Europe during the 8th, 9th, 10th and 11th centuries.

Wrath
Anger.